THE
TOTALLY NINJA
RACCOONS
MEET THE
JERSEY DEVIL

by Kevin Coolidge

Illustrated by Jubal Lee

Be a read.ng ninja!

Jim Coly

The Totally Ninja Raccoons Are:

Rascal:
He's the shortest brother and loves doughnuts. He's great with his paws and makes really cool gadgets. He's a little goofy and loves both his brothers, even when they pick on him, but maybe not right then.

Bandit:
He's the oldest brother. He's tall and lean. He's super smart and loves to read. He leads the Totally Ninja Raccoons, but he couldn't do it by himself.

Kevin:
He may be the middle brother, but he refuses to be stuck in the middle. He has the moves and the street smarts that the Totally Ninja Raccoons are going to need, even if it does sometimes get them into trouble as well as out of trouble.

CONTENTS

1. One Track Mind   page 1

2. A Plan is Hatched   page 7

3. Phantom of the Pines   page 11

4. Living Legend   page 15

5. Breakfast of Champions   page 21

6. Huck and Finn Are In   page 27

7. Animal Land   page 33

8. What the Devil?   page 39

9. Good Bye Devil   page 43

"What are these tracks here?" asks Kevin as he points
to a set of tracks behind them.

1

ONE TRACK MIND

Fat, fluffy flakes fill the sky. The Totally Ninja Raccoons are exploring the Pine Creek Rail Trail just outside of Wellsboro, Pennsylvania. Bandit and Kevin glide across the trail on cross-country skis, and Rascal tromps along on snowshoes.

"Cross-country skiing is great exercise. It builds strength, agility, and balance. Just what ninjas need," says Bandit.

"I prefer snow shoes. It's easier to learn, and better for carrying a load," says Rascal.

"The Pine Creek Trail is a great place for both," says Kevin.

"With all this fresh snow, snowshoes are the better choice for you, Rascal, especially with that heavy pack," replies Bandit.

"I need to carry my tools and snacks. Ninjas need snacks," says Rascal.

"Ninjas also need to have rest," says Kevin.

"And food for energy. Is it snack time yet?" asks Rascal.

The tallest brother stops and rests his paws on his hips. "I suppose we can take a break for water and a protein bar," says Bandit.

Rascal rubs his paws together. "I brought birch beer and doughnuts!" he says.

"Hmmm, I sure could use some hot chocolate right about now," says Kevin.

"I don't think ninja leaders eat doughnuts," says Bandit.

"That's more doughnuts for us!" chirps Rascal.

Rascal drops his backpack beside a fallen log, and plops down. He opens the pack and brings out three cans of birch beer and a box of doughnuts.

"I can't believe someone threw out these powdered pastries," says Rascal.

"Toss me a birch beer, bro," says Kevin.

Bandit just shakes his furry head and says,"When you two stop feeding your faces, I want you to take a look around. A ninja needs to be aware."

Kevin pops open a can of birch beer. "I'm aware of being thirsty," says Kevin.

"I'm aware of being hungry," says Rascal as he crams an entire doughnut into his furry face. Powdered sugar coats his whiskers.

"I mean to be aware of your surroundings," says Bandit.

"We're in the Pennsylvania Grand Canyon on the Pine Creek Rail Trail. I thought you knew that," says Kevin.

"I could draw you a map. I have my colored pencils in my backpack somewhere," says Rascal.

"It's quiet. We're the only ones out here tonight," says Kevin.

"Ha, but are we? Look there, behind the log. See those long oval tracks with the two round circles?" asks Bandit.

Bandit takes a book out of his pack. It's the *Field Guide to Tracking Animals in Snow*. "Those are the tracks of a rabbit."

"That bunny is long gone though," says Rascal.

"See how crisp the edges are? There's snow falling, and there's very little in the print. These tracks are fresh," said Bandit.

"Why do we want to track a rabbit?" asks Kevin.

"It's good to know what's been here," said Bandit.

Bandit holds out the book, turns the page and shows it to Rascal and Kevin. "See these paw prints and how they make a straight line? Those belong to *Felis domesticus*."

"Oh, that sounds scary!" exclaims Rascal.

"That just means a common house cat," says Kevin.

"Gypsy, head of the Cat Board, is a house cat, and she's scary," says Rascal.

"Exactly. If you observe your surroundings, they will tell you everything you need to know," says Bandit.

"What are those prints near the water?" asks Kevin.

"Those are otter prints. You can see otters in Pine Creek sometimes," says Bandit.

"Oh, this is fun. What are those little prints over there?" asks Rascal.

"Hmmm, see the tiny toenails? That's probably a deer mouse, and see that dent? It looks like a bird of prey caught him," says Bandit.

"Like our friend the thunderbird?" asks Rascal.

"Well, a LOT smaller, probably a red-tailed hawk, or a great horned owl, but it's hard to tell," says Bandit.

"Cool, what are these tracks here?" asks Kevin as he points to a set of tracks behind them.

"They are small and come to a point. They look a little like goat prints, but are too small," says Bandit.

"They go back the way we just came, but they stop right here," says Rascal.

"No, they start up again right here," says Kevin as he points to the snow several feet in front of them.

"That's silly. They can't do that," says Bandit.

Rascal adjusts his glasses and points, "There are more along the railing of the bridge."

Bandit quickly turns the pages of the book. "There's nothing in the book that matches them."

A blood-curdling scream cuts through the night, and a swish of wings. "What was that?!" shouts Kevin.

"There it is! It looks like a kangaroo with a goat's head!" shouts Rascal.

"That's impossible! It must be an owl," says Kevin.

"No, I think Rascal just saw the famous Jersey Devil!" says Bandit.

"What's the Jersey Devil?" asks Rascal.

"It's the hockey team that the Pittsburgh Penguins beat all the time," says Kevin.

"No, the Jersey Devil is a legendary creature said to inhabit the Pine Barrens of Southern New Jersey," says Bandit.

"What's it doing in north-central Pennsylvania?"

"That is a good question," says Bandit.

"Looking for a hockey game?" says Kevin.

"We need to look into this," says Bandit.

"We need to go home. I'm totally out of snacks," says Rascal.

"Let's go back. I need to read up on the Jersey Devil," says Bandit.

Kevin sighs, "The Jersey Devil is in the details."

"We need a new plan to take care of the
Totally Ninja Raccoons."

2

A PLAN IS HATCHED

Earlier that day at the hidden location of the Cat Board, that super-secret organization made up of cats that want to take over the world...

Several cats are softly talking among themselves. An all black cat grooms his tail. A plump calico cat sits at a table. She glares at the other cats, and thumps a gavel on the table.

"Silence! It's time to get this meeting started. Huck, read the minutes from the last meeting," yowls Gypsy.

A black and white cat looks up, "Forty-three minutes," meows Huck.

A large Siamese cat looks irritated and yowls. "No, minutes from a meeting means what happened at the last meeting," says the Siamese cat.

"Finn farted," laughs Huck.

"This meeting will come to order!" meows Gypsy.

"I'll take a T-bone steak, medium rare, please," says Huck.

Finn, the cat as black as midnight, licks his lips and paws and purrs, "It's Friday, and that means fish fry. I like extra tartar sauce with mine."

A nearly hairless cat speaks up. It's a sphinx. "We need to take care of business. Those Totally Ninja Raccoons keep spoiling our plans for world domination!"

"I think Finn's butt is spoiled. I can smell his stinky bum from here," laughs Huck.

"You are just jealous. You are a bad hunter, and must be fed by your humans," says Finn.

A little black and white cat that looks like she's wearing a tuxedo speaks up. It's Velvet. "Eating fish out of a trash can is NOT hunting. I am a great hunter."

"What do you hunt?" asks Huck.

"I hunt moles," says Velvet proudly.

"Do they taste good?" asks Finn.

"No, they taste like dirt," says Velvet.

A big fluffy Persian cat meows, "We need a new plan to take care of the Totally Ninja Raccoons."

"I knew Gypsy's last plan wouldn't work. I think it's time for new leadership. I nominate... me!" says the Siamese cat.

"Not so fast! I founded the Cat Board, and I have a great idea. I know someone who knows someone who knows someone," said Gypsy.

"You've said that before," says the Siamese cat.

"This is fool-proof. I've heard of a legendary creature that works cheap. He'll take care of our Ninja Raccoon problem," says Gypsy.

"What is this 'creature' you speak of?" asked the Persian cat.

"He's a living legend in New Jersey," says Gypsy.

"New Jersey? Forget about it. You have to be kidding me?" says the Siamese cat.

"None other than the Jersey Devil!" meows Gypsy.

"I love hockey!" says Huck.

"Jersey Devil? What is the Jersey Devil?" asks the Siamese cat.

"Awww, you just saw an owl carrying a mouse,"
says Kevin.

3

PHANTOM OF THE PINES

Kevin thrusts and pokes with his staff. Bandit reads from a book called *Phantom of the Pines*. Rascal tinkers at a table filled with tools.

Bandit points to a page. "It says right here that the Jersey Devil is often described as a flying biped with hooves."

"Good bye and good riddance is what I say," says Kevin.

"No, a biped is an animal that uses two legs for walking," says Bandit.

"Or running, but I can't run fast. I have short legs," says Rascal.

"The creature is usually described as having the head of a goat, bat-like wings, small arms with claws, a forked tail, and emits a 'blood-curdling' scream," says Bandit.

"That's it! That's what I saw!" yells Rascal.

"Awww, you just saw an owl carrying a mouse," says Kevin.

"You heard it too!" yells Rascal.

"It was a screech owl," says Kevin.

"There have been sightings going back hundreds of years. There are even photos," says Bandit.

Rascal shows Bandit and Kevin a photo of the Jersey Devil on the front cover of the *Wellsboro Gazette*. "Like this one? I told you I saw something," says Rascal.

"It's a hoax. It's not real," says Kevin.

Bandit grabs the paper and reads the headline, **"Jersey Devil Spotted on Pine Creek Trail!"**

"He wasn't spotted. He was brown and furry," says Rascal.

"The editor is claiming the Jersey Devil was seen, or maybe someone took a photo of a fake. It can't be real," says Kevin.

"The editor is calling the Jersey Devil a menace to society and is offering a reward for the creature if captured alive," says Bandit.

"He just wants to sell newspapers. I bet he faked the photo himself," says Kevin.

"The editor claims to have seen the creature himself. He swears it's not a fake," says Bandit.

"He sold a lot of papers when our friend Nessie was on the front page," says Kevin.

"And we know that Nessie is real," says Bandit.

"If the Jersey Devil is real, and the newspaper works

up enough people, that devil is going to end up in a cage at Animal Land," says Kevin.

"I hate cages. We have to warn the Jersey Devil," says Rascal.

"How much is the reward anyway?" asks Kevin.

"Kevin!" yell Bandit and Rascal.

"Just kidding! I hate cages too," says Kevin.

"We need to find the Jersey Devil before the humans do!" yells Rascal.

"What is the Jersey Devil's favorite snack food?" asks Kevin.

"Well, I haven't gotten that far in the book, and I'm more familiar with Pennsylvania snacks," says Bandit.

"No, it's a joke," says Kevin.

"Being locked up in a cage is no joke, Kevin. We were lucky enough to escape Animal Land." says Bandit.

"Ghoul Scout cookies! Get it?" asks Kevin.

"I don't get it?" says Rascal.

"Let's get to it, Ninja Raccoons," says Bandit.

Bandit and Rascal grab their backpacks and run out the door. Kevin grabs a can of birch beer and stuffs it into his backpack.

"Ghoul Scouts sound like Girl Scouts...no one gets my jokes," grumbles Kevin.

"How you doing? This is a nice place you got here,"
says the Jersey Devil.

4

LIVING LEGEND

The infamous Cat Board assembles in their headquarters, which is a cave so super-secret no one knows about it, except the Cat Board, and the Totally Ninja Raccoons who have been there before. Rascal even has a map.

Velvet shakes snow off her whiskers. "I'm glad we are able to use the cave. It's cold outside."

"Yes, so glad to be rid of that pesky unicorn," says Gypsy.

The Siamese looks disgusted and flicks multicolored specks off her fur. "I just wish we could get rid of this glitter."

"Glitter is forever!" meows Huck.

The nearly hairless Sphinx Cat sits up tall and speaks, "Meow, it was me who convinced the little green men to take the unicorn with them."

"The Cat Board is lucky to have such a smart member like... me. So good. I'm super smart," says Gypsy.

"Then tell us more about this Jersey Devil and your plan to totally get rid of those Ninja Raccoons," says the Persian cat.

Gypsy rubs her paws together, and points her fat paw towards the entrance of the cave. "I'll do more than that. Here he is to tell you himself," yowls Gypsy.

A gust of wind sends flakes of snow and glitter flying around the cave. In comes a strange looking creature. "How you doing? This is a nice place you got here," says the Jersey Devil.

"So, tell us about this plan of yours to rid us of these Totally Ninja Raccoons. Ahh, Mr. Devil," says the Siamese Cat.

"You can call me Tony," says the Jersey Devil.

"Yes, please be frank. We have nibbles to nibble and naps to take," says the Siamese cat.

"I'm Tony, not Frank, and I'll get right to the point. I'll trap these raccoons and make 'em disappear," says the Jersey Devil.

The Persian cat sniffs, "We've heard that before."

"I always do the job I'm paid for. Speaking of which, when do I see the denaro?" says Tony the Devil.

"Denaro?" questions Finn.

"The money. I need paid for my services. Money, it doesn't grow on trees," says Tony.

"Money is made from paper," says Huck.

"Actually, money is made of cotton and linen," says Finn.

"How do you even know that?" asks Huck.

"I've been reading. I'm thinking of selling my collection of fish heads, and I want to get good money for them," says Finn.

Gypsy looks disgusted at the mention of money. "Money? I have something much better than money."

"What's better than money?" says the Jersey Devil.

"Favor with the Cat Board. We are going to rule the world, and we can make this worth your while," says Gypsy.

"Hmmm, I've always wanted to own my own state. How about I do this thing? You give me New Jersey?" says Tony, the Jersey Devil.

"Done!" yells Gypsy.

"You do know that Pennsylvania is basically land-locked? We are going to need a seaport?" sniffs the Persian cat.

"We'll have New York City and the West Coast. You can't make an omelet without breaking a few eggs," says Gypsy.

"I like my eggs scrambled," says Huck.

"Dippy eggs!" yells Finn.

"With bacon!" yells Huck.

"All this talk of food is making me hungry," says the Sphinx cat.

"Yes, it is time to get to the eating portion of the meeting. Take care of the Ninja Raccoons and New Jersey is yours, Devil," says Gypsy.

"Tony, you can call me Tony. We're on a first name basis here," says Tony.

"Time to fill my belly!" says Finn.

The Cat Board breaks out the snacks. The Jersey Devil rubs his hands together, the claws clicking and smiles. "Jersey is going to be mine. There's going to be some changes. I'm going to take care of these raccoons my way."

"The devil! I saw the Jersey Devil last night, and he set my pants on fire!" yells the man.

5

BREAKFAST OF CHAMPIONS

A man slumps on his stool at the counter at the famous Wellsboro Diner. His hands shake as he brings the cup of coffee to his mouth. He sets the coffee cup back down and stuffs a doughnut into his mouth. Crumbs fall onto his wrinkled tie. He brushes them off and pulls out a pack of cigarettes. He searches his pockets for a lighter.

"There's no smoking in the Diner. Besides, those things will kill you," says the waitress.

"Ha, I almost died last night. I stared into the abyss, and the abyss burned my pants! I can't find my lighter anyway," says the man.

"I don't know what that means," says the waitress.

"The devil! I saw the Jersey Devil last night, and he set my pants on fire!" yells the man.

An old man with a beard laughs, "Didn't bother to change your pants before breakfast?"

"I was hungry, and I needed to write the follow-up to my article for the paper. This beast must be stopped!" yells the man.

A chuckle comes from the corner, "Liar, liar, pants on fire? You still yapping about that...what do you call it?" says the old man with glasses.

"The Jersey Devil! Ha, you have to be kidding me. Wellsboro is miles away from Jersey. No self-respecting devil is going to be in Canyon Country. You sure you didn't see a Sidehill Gouger?" laughs an old man with a shiny bald spot.

The old man with the glasses takes a sip of coffee, "Everyone knows the Jersey Devil is a Pine Barren creature. Ain't no pine barrens 'round here."

The editor wipes powder from his chin and takes a big gulp of coffee. "I'm telling you I saw the Jersey Devil. I was walking home after work. I was strolling across the Green, and the Devil swooped out of the shadows and started chasing me!"

The old, bald man says, "You sure you just didn't see one of those statues?"

"The Devil burned my pants!" yells the man.

The old man with the glasses laughs. "You sure it wasn't one of those pesky raccoons you keep writing about? Maybe they stole your cigarette lighter too?"

"Those raccoons are a menace. They steal my garbage. We totally need to catch them and send them back to Animal Land. But this creature had glowing eyes, and that scream! It was like nothing I've ever heard," says the editor.

"You ever hear a screech owl, city man?" asks the old man with a beard.

The old man with a shiny bald spot says, "I heard a mountain lion when I was young. Sounds just like a woman screaming."

"Or maybe the editor of the paper screaming," laughs the old man with the glasses.

All three men laugh and order more coffee.

"I'm serious. I'm doubling the reward for his capture," says the editor.

The old man with a beard laughs and points. "Maybe you ought to save your money, and buy yourself a pair of new pants."

A tall, lean man with a baseball cap turns from his seat at the counter and looks at the editor. "I could catch this Jersey Devil."

"Finally, someone who knows their civic duty. I'll make you famous. I'll put your photo in the paper. I'll write an article you can cut out and save for your grandchildren," says the man.

The old man with a beard laughs. "Oh, don't let him fool you. No one reads the *Wellsboro Gazette* anymore, not after the case of the missing statue."

The old man with the glasses exclaims, "I do! I loved the article on the fake Loch Ness monster. Ain't no way that small lake holds a sea monster."

The man with the shiny bald spot says, "You read?"

"Every day," says the old man with the glasses.

The tall, lean man stands up and puts some money on the counter. "I've tracked this devil all the way from Jersey. I'll capture him, but I'm selling him to the highest bidder."

"A creature like that needs to be in a cage. It's dangerous. He burned my pants!" yells the man.

"I'll take care of it," says the tall, lean man.

"I'd pay good money to see such a creature," says the old man with a beard.

"I sure hope Animal Land gets it," says the old man with a shiny bald spot.

"We could poke it with a stick and get an ice cream," says the old man with the glasses.

The tall, lean man saunters out of the Diner.

25

"Gypsy will never give up her idea of world domination."

6

HUCK AND FINN ARE IN

The Totally Ninja Raccoons slink across Wellsboro's Green.

"It's good to see the statue back where it belongs," says Rascal.

"I kind of liked the big empty hole in the middle of the Green," says Kevin.

"We were blamed for the theft and we put things right, made a new friend, and stopped the evil plot of the Cat Board," says Bandit.

"Speaking of the Cat Board... I wonder what Gypsy is up to?" asks Kevin.

A voice from the shadows speaks, "Meow, she's up to no good."

"As usual," says a second voice.

Huck and Finn step from the shadows.

"Is Gypsy trying to take over the world?" asks Rascal.

"Again," says Kevin.

"Gypsy will never give up her idea of world domination, but she's convinced she has to get rid of you, the..." says Huck.

"Totally!" shouts Rascal.

"Ninja!" shouts Kevin.

"Raccoons!" shouts Bandit.

"Exactly," says Finn.

"We aren't going anywhere, except maybe back to bed. There are way too many people out and about for this time of night," says Kevin.

"We couldn't even get any General Tso's chicken at the Dumpling House, or raid the trash cans of the editor's house," says Rascal.

"I counted 24 traps, and I suspect the pork-fried rice has sleeping pills in it," says Bandit.

"I am feeling kind of tired," says Rascal.

"You didn't???" says Kevin.

"I just ate all the pork out of it. I was hungry," says Rascal.

"So, do you know why all these people are out at this time of night, Huck and Finn?" asks Bandit.

"They are looking for the Jersey Devil. The editor of the paper is offering a huge reward for his capture," answers Huck.

"Is he lost? What's the Jersey Devil doing so far from New Jersey?" asks Rascal.

"Gypsy convinced him to help get rid of the Ninja Raccoons," says Finn.

"I knew he was outside his usual habitat, though he has been sighted in southern Pennsylvania," says Bandit.

"Why are you telling us this? Aren't you members of the Cat Board?" asks Kevin.

"We consider ourselves free agents. If you want loyalty, buy a dog. I'm there because of Finn, and Finn is there because of snacks," says Huck.

"Do they serve birch beer? I could use a cold birch beer," says Rascal.

"We know!" shout Kevin and Bandit.

"Sometimes the barn cats deliver milk," says Finn, licking his chops.

"So, why are you here?" asks Bandit.

"What these humans don't know yet is that the Jersey Devil has been captured, and taken to Animal Land. I thought you could help us free him," says Huck.

"I don't see why," says Kevin.

"I can't go back to Animal Land. I won't!" yells Rascal.

"That's exactly why we should. The Jersey Devil is thought to be a myth. If he's proven to be real, and put on display, then what of the other creatures? Like our friend Bigfoot, or Nessie, or the thunderbird?" says Bandit.

"Exactly, it will bring so many people to Wellsboro that we will never be able to cross the road," says Finn.

"Or explore the town at night, and get into the dumpsters," says Rascal.

"We could catch up on our sleep?" says Kevin.

"Kevin! Let's free the Jersey Devil and send a message to Gypsy and the editor of the Wellsboro Gazette," says Bandit.

"I could draw the editor a map to go with the message?" says Rascal.

"I could tell him where to go," says Kevin.

"We're going to free the Jersey Devil!" yell Huck and Finn.

"I don't see why we can't just watch a hockey game and watch the Philadelphia Flyers beat the Jersey Devils," pouts Kevin.

"I never should have fallen for the Mallomars.
Oldest trick in the book,"

7

ANIMAL LAND

Five shadows creep through the darkness of the night. The Totally Ninja Raccoons and Huck and Finn sneak through Animal Land.

"We need to find the cage the Jersey Devil is in, and release him," says Bandit.

Rascal sniffs the air. "Can we stop by the snack bar first?"

"Did you say snack bar? I could use a snack," says Finn.

"We do the job first, then we have a snack," says Huck.

"I say we grab a burger, and then we call it a night. My bed is calling me," says Kevin.

"The Jersey Devil is counting on us!" says Huck.

"Quiet, what was that?" says Bandit.

"Oh, I farted. I had fish for dinner," says Finn.

"Everything makes you fart," says Huck.

"Why are we releasing the Jersey Devil again?" asks Finn.

"I told you. If the Jersey Devil is real, people will come for miles around, and we'll never be able to do cat and raccoon things," says Huck.

"And I don't want the editor proven right. He got my bad side the last time he took my photo," says Kevin.

"We release the Jersey Devil, show up the editor, and save Wellsboro for the animals," says Huck.

"All the animals," says Rascal.

The Ninja Raccoons and the cats glide through the zoo. There's a mountain lion pacing in a cage, a bear snores, and there's an empty cage that reads: "Raccoons."

Rascal shivers and keeps walking. The party comes to a covered cage. A strange muttering comes from inside.

"I never should have fallen for the Mallomars. Oldest trick in the book," says the voice.

"What is a Mallomar?" whispers Kevin.

"Round graham crackers topped with marshmallow and covered in dark chocolate," says the voice.

"Oh, those sound yummy! I bet they would be great with a birch beer!" says Rascal.

"What is a birch beer?" says the voice.

"It's a carbonated soft drink made from birch extract," says Bandit.

"You are pulling my forked tail," says the voice.

"No, really. It's my favorite soda," says Rascal.

"Well, get me out of this cage and we'll go get some," says the voice.

"And Mallomars?" asks Rascal.

"Sure, if we can get them around here," says the voice.

Kevin grabs the cloth and pulls it off, and there is the Jersey Devil.

"Now, we need to get him out," says Bandit.

Huck steps forward. "This is where I come in."

Huck pops a claw and picks the lock.

"Let's get out of here," says the Jersey Devil.

"Wait a minute. I have an idea. Let's put everything back the way we found it," says Kevin.

"I am NOT getting back into that cage," huffs the Jersey Devil.

"No, we create the illusion of putting everything back, including a copy of the Jersey Devil," says Bandit.

"If I had enough time, I could build a robot," says Rascal.

"Could you have it breathe fire?" asks the Jersey Devil.

"Yes, I could even get it to fly. If I can borrow Bandit's books on rockets," says Rascal.

"You know you can borrow my books any time," says Bandit.

"That's great, but we are running out of time," says Huck.

"We can make a snow angel!" shouts Finn.

"Or a snow devil!" laughs the Jersey Devil.

Everyone grabs some snow and begins to build a snow devil.

"I'll grab some pine branches for the wings," says Rascal.

The gang finishes building the snow devil.

"Now, put the cover back on, and let's get back to the clubhouse," says Bandit.

"That just about covers it," says Huck.

"Hey, that was my line!" shouts Kevin.

"Totally," says Rascal.

"Do we have time to stop at the snack bar?" asks Finn.

"The Jersey Devil, he's gone!"
shouts the editor.

8

WHAT THE DEVIL?

Huge eyes stare out of a pair of binoculars. It's Gypsy and the members of the Cat Board watching Animal Land.

"I knew we should have gotten someone else," says Gypsy.

"It was your idea to hire the Jersey Devil," says the Persian cat.

"Well, at least we didn't pay him," says the Siamese cat.

"Where are Huck and Finn?" says the Sphinx cat.

"They said something about hunting," says Velvet.

A large group of humans are gathered around the cage. The editor of the paper is there smiling with his camera. "This is history in the making!

The legendary Jersey Devil will be exposed to the world!"

"I'll be famous... and rich. Don't forget my check," says the tall, lean man.

"My legacy is complete. I'll sell a million papers!" says the editor.

"Ladies and gentlemen, I present you the mysterious creature, the phantom of the pines, exclusive to Wellsboro's very own Animal Land!" shouts the editor.

The editor grabs the cloth and pulls, revealing the snowman shaped like the Jersey Devil.

"It's a hoax!" shouts the old man with a beard.

"You pulled me away from my bacon and eggs for this?" says the old man with the shiny bald spot.

"I need another cup of coffee, and this week's paper. I got a great photo. Maybe I can sell it to the editor?" says the old man with the glasses.

"I'll still be needing that check," says the tall, lean man.

"The Jersey Devil, he's gone!" shouts the editor.

"I delivered what was promised. Not my fault he got away," says the tall, lean man.

"I'm ruined!" shouts the editor.

"They always say the Jersey Devil is in the details," laughs the old man with the beard.

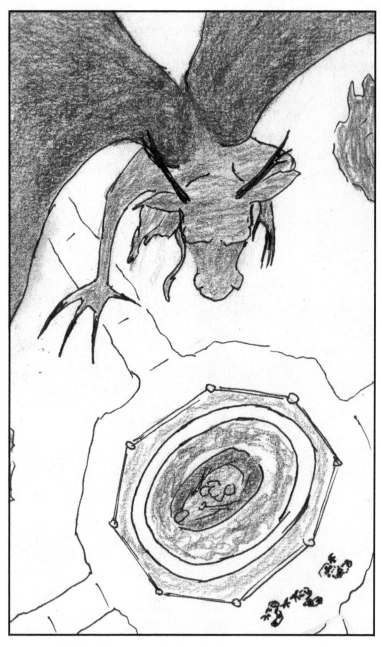

"Thanks so much for helping me escape,"
says the Jersey Devil.

9

GOOD BYE DEVIL

The Totally Ninja Raccoons are at the Green with Huck, Finn, and the Jersey Devil.

"Thanks so much for helping me escape," says the Jersey Devil.

"You are welcome. I hope you enjoyed Wellsboro, Mr. Devil," says Bandit.

"I didn't get to see as much as I would have liked, and you can call me Tony. We're friends now," says Tony, the Jersey Devil.

"You'll have to come back in the spring, Tony," says Rascal.

"Or the fall. Tioga County is known for its fall foliage," says Finn.

"That's leaves. We have really pretty leaves," says Huck.

"I'll be back," says Tony, the Jersey Devil.

"Bring some of those Mallomars," says Rascal.

"I will," says Tony.

The Jersey Devil scampers away, making tracks across the Green and up Wynken, Blyken and Nod. He reaches Wynken's head and then takes flight into the night.

"I'm going to miss Tony," says Rascal.

"We're going to miss supper," says Kevin.

"Our rural town is now quiet and peaceful. Now, let's hit the Chinese restaurant," says Bandit.

"Totally," says Kevin and Rascal.

"Can we come too?" ask Huck and Finn.

"There's always room for friends," says Bandit.

The Totally Ninja Raccoons jump into the air and slap their paws together, "We are the Totally Ninja Raccoons!"

"And Huck and Finn too!" shout Huck and Finn.

"I sure hope there are fish heads," says Finn.

THE END

The Pine Creek Rail Trail

The Pine Creek Rail Trail is located just outside Wellsboro, Pennsylvania. The trail runs through the Pine Creek Gorge, also known as the "Grand Canyon of Pennsylvania". Here you can bike, hike, cross-country ski, or snowshoe through some of Pennsylvania's most beautiful scenery.

The trail is a converted railroad track that was once used during the lumber era of the region. The trail is now protected by the National Park Service and trail users can view waterfalls and wildlife like deer, river otters, black bear, bald eagles and more.

The trail is well-maintained and mostly composed of gravel. There are many access points to this 62-mile trail, making it easy to plan an outing of almost any distance. The scenery is amazing. You won't be disappointed by taking this great trail. Visit **www.wellsboropa.com** for more information.

The Jersey Devil

The Jersey Devil is a legendary creature said to live in the Pine Barrens of southern New Jersey. The creature is described as a flying biped with hooves. The description is that of a kangaroo-like creature with the head of a goat, bat wings, small arms with clawed hands, and a forked tail.

There have been many claims and sightings involving the Jersey Devil. It has been reported to move quickly and often is described as emitting a "blood-curdling" scream. According to popular folklore, the Jersey Devil was born on a stormy night to a human woman.

Born as a normal baby, the cursed child changed to a strange creature. Growling and screaming, it flew up the chimney and headed into the Pine Barrens.

Many people believe the Jersey Devil is nothing more than a story to scare children, but other people have claimed to have seen the creature. Is the Jersey Devil real? Or is it just a story and legend? Read more, become a reading ninja, and decide for yourself.

About the Author

Kevin resides in Wellsboro, just a short hike from the Pennsylvania Grand Canyon. When he's not writing, you can find him at *From My Shelf Books & Gifts*, an independent bookstore he runs with his lovely wife, several helpful employees, and two friendly cats, Huck & Finn.

He's recently become an honorary member of the Cat Board, and when he's not scooping the litter box, or feeding Gypsy her tuna, he's writing more stories about the Totally Ninja Raccoons. Be sure to catch their next big adventure, *The Totally Ninja Raccoons Discover the Lost World.*

You can write him at:

From My Shelf Books & Gifts
7 East Ave., Suite 101
Wellsboro, PA 16901

www.wellsborobookstore.com

About the Illustrator

Jubal Lee is a former Wellsboro resident who now resides in sunny Florida, due to his extreme allergic reaction to cold weather.

He is an eclectic artist who, when not drawing raccoons, werewolves, and the like, enjoys writing, bicycling, and short walks on the beach.

Get your own copies of the adventures with the Totally Ninja Raccoons!

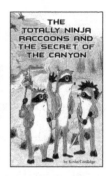

THE TOTALLY NINJA RACCOONS MEET BIGFOOT
by Kevin Coolidge

THE TOTALLY NINJA RACCOONS MEET THE WEIRD & WACKY WEREWOLF
by Kevin Coolidge

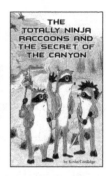

THE TOTALLY NINJA RACCOONS AND THE SECRET OF THE CANYON
by Kevin Coolidge

THE TOTALLY NINJA RACCOONS MEET THE THUNDERBIRD
by Kevin Coolidge

THE TOTALLY NINJA RACCOONS AND THE CATMAS CAPER

THE TOTALLY NINJA RACCOONS AND THE SECRET OF NESSMUK LAKE
by Kevin Coolidge

THE TOTALLY NINJA RACCOONS MEET THE LITTLE GREEN MEN
by Kevin Coolidge

THE TOTALLY NINJA RACCOONS MEET THE JERSEY DEVIL
by Kevin Coolidge

The Totally Ninja Raccoons Meet Bigfoot

_____ copies @ $5.99 each = _____

The Totally Ninja Raccoons Meet the Weird & Wacky Werewolf

_____ copies @ $5.99 each = _____

The Totally Ninja Raccoons and the Secret of the Canyon

_____ copies @ $5.99 each = _____

The Totally Ninja Raccoons Meet the Thunderbird

_____ copies @ $5.99 each = _____

The Totally Ninja Raccoons and the Catmas Caper

_____ copies @ $6.99 each = _____

The Totally Ninja Raccoons and the Secret of Nessmuk Lake

_____ copies @ $6.99 each = _____

The Totally Ninja Raccoons Meet the Little Green Men

_____ copies @ $6.99 each = _____

The Totally Ninja Raccoons Meet the Jersey Devil

_____ copies @ $6.99 each = _____

Subtotal = _____

$2.99 shipping = _____
(15 books or less)

Total Enclosed = _____

Send this form, with payment via check or money order, to:
From My Shelf Books & Gifts
7 East Ave., Suite 101
Wellsboro, PA 16901

or call **(570) 724-5793**
Also available at **wellsborobookstore.com**